Written by Joe Fitzpatrick

Illustrated by Marco Furlotti

Designed by Flowerpot Press
in Franklin, TN.
www.FlowerpotPress.com
Designer: Stephanie Meyers
Editor: Katrine Crow
ROR-0811-0112
ISBN: 978-1-4867-1266-3
Made in China/Fabriqué en Chine

It's time for bed.
I want a book.
And I want you to read it.

But listen close to my advice,
you are gonna need it.

This book is not like other books
that we have read before.

It looks the same as normal books,
but it has one rule more...

Whisper when you read this book.
It's safer when you're quiet.

One time I read this book out loud
and that started a riot.

Whisper when you read this book.
If others want to hear...

have them cuddle in real close,
then whisper in their ear.

Whisper when you read this book.
It makes the book more fun.

It also means I listen close
until the book is done.

Whisper when you read this book.
I won't make a peep.

Don't worry if my eyes are closed.
I am not asleep.

Whisper when you read this book.
Get in nice and tight.

And when you're done
say "I love you,"
then kiss my head good night.

20941

Riding the Ferry with Captain Cruz

**Written by
ALICE K. FLANAGAN**

**Photographs by
CHRISTINE OSINSKI**

Reading Consultant
LINDA CORNWELL
Learning Resource Consultant
Indiana Department Of Education

CHILDREN'S PRESS®   *A Division of Grolier Publishing*
New York • London • Hong Kong • Sydney • Danbury, Connecticut

Special thanks to Daniel Cruz
for allowing us to tell his story.

Also, thanks to Captain Mauldin and
the New York Department of Transportation.

Library of Congress Cataloging-in-Publication Data

Flanagan, Alice.

    Riding the ferry with Captain Cruz / by Alice K. Flanagan; photographs by Christine Osinski.

      p.   cm. — (Our neighborhood)

    Summary: Simple text and photographs describe the duties and responsibilities of Captain Cruz, a ferry boat captain who takes people back and forth from Staten Island to New York City.

    ISBN: 0-516-20046-1 (lib. bdg.)—0-516-26059-6 (pbk.)

    1. Ferries—New York (State)—Staten Island—Juvenile literature. [1. Ship captains. 2. Occupations. 3. Staten Island Ferry. 4. Ferries.] I. Osinski, Christine, ill. II. Title. III. Series: Our neighborhood (New York, N.Y.)

    VM421.F55 1996

    386'.6'0974726—dc20   96-17145

                                                        CIP

                                                         AC

Photographs ©: Christine Osinski

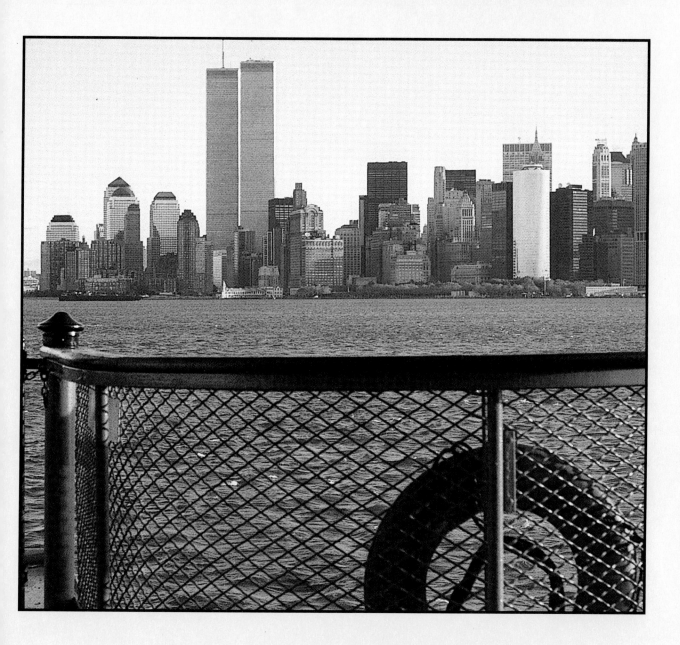

Hear the horn blow?
Hurry!
The ferryboat is leaving.

See the captain on deck?
That's Mr. Cruz, my neighbor.

All day long, Captain Cruz takes people back and forth from Staten Island to New York City, across the bay.

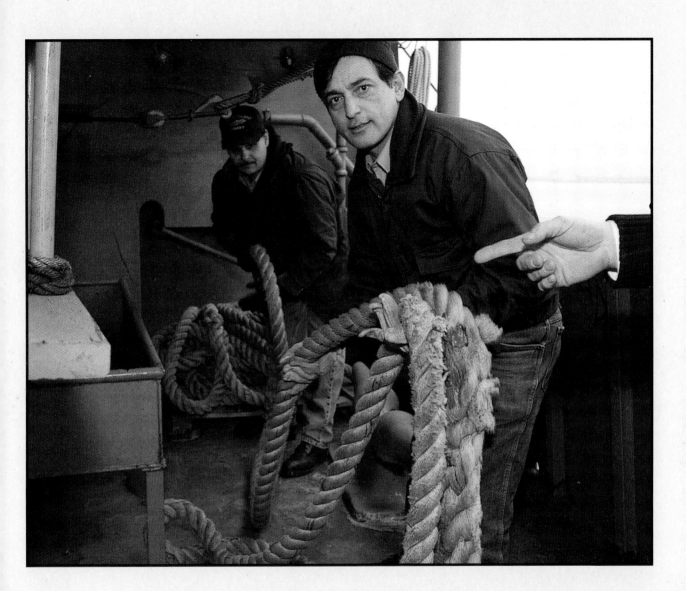

Before the ferry leaves,
the crew makes sure everything
on board works.
The trip must be safe!

Hear the engines hum?

Slowly, Captain Cruz steers the ferry away from the dock.

He checks his compass to see
which direction the ferry is going.

He watches the radar screen.
It shows him how to keep the
ferry on course.

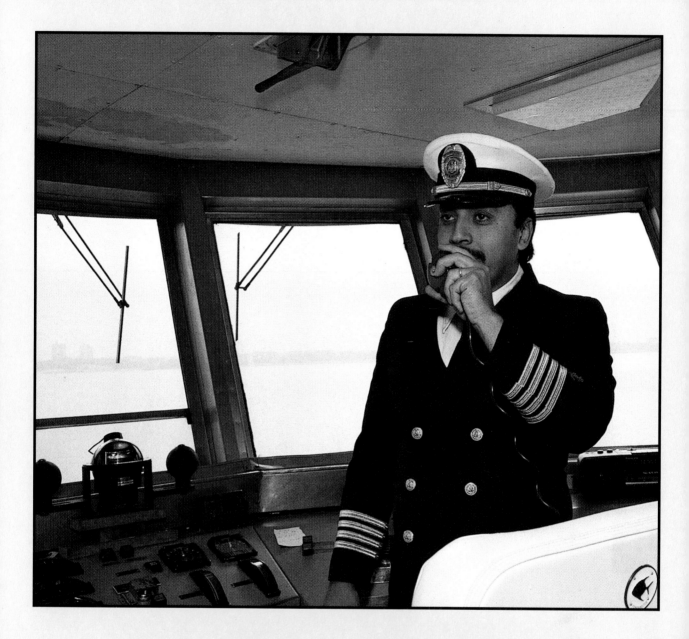

Captain Cruz uses a radio to talk
with his crew.
They are like a family.

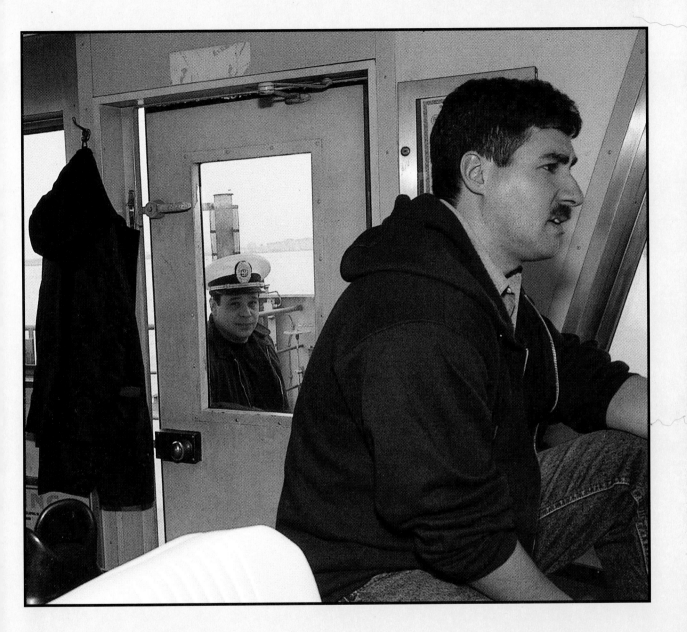

A deck hand sits at the captain's
side day and night.
He is an extra pair of eyes
looking out.

Feel the roll of the waves?

The captain handles the ferry well.
He has been a ferryboat captain for
ten years.

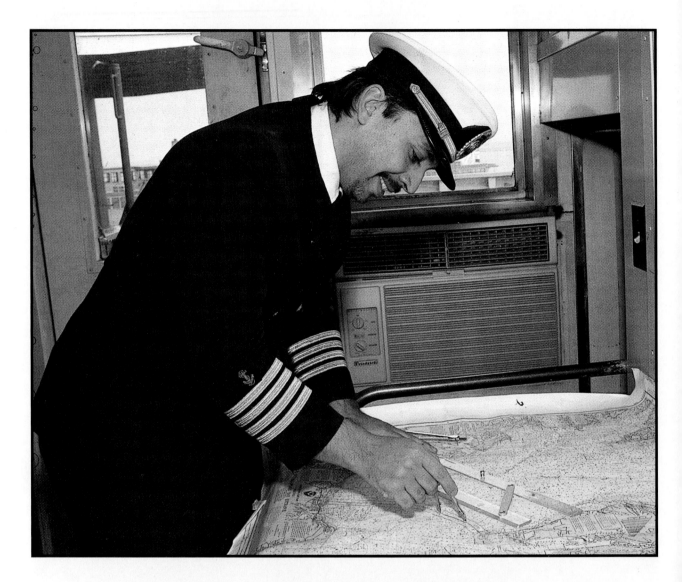

He knows all about
the weather and the water currents,

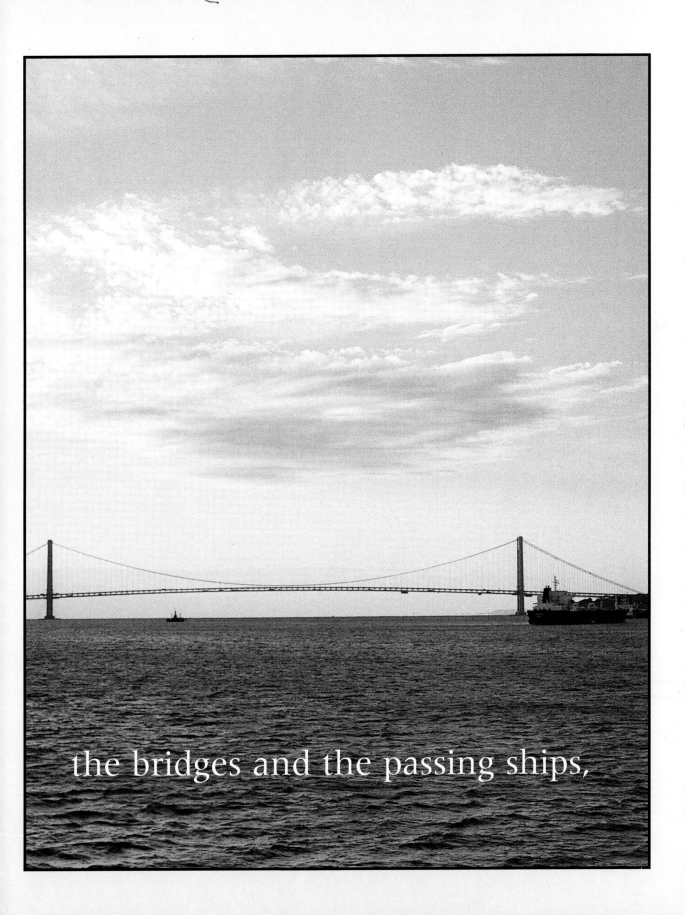

the bridges and the passing ships,

and the famous Statue of Liberty.

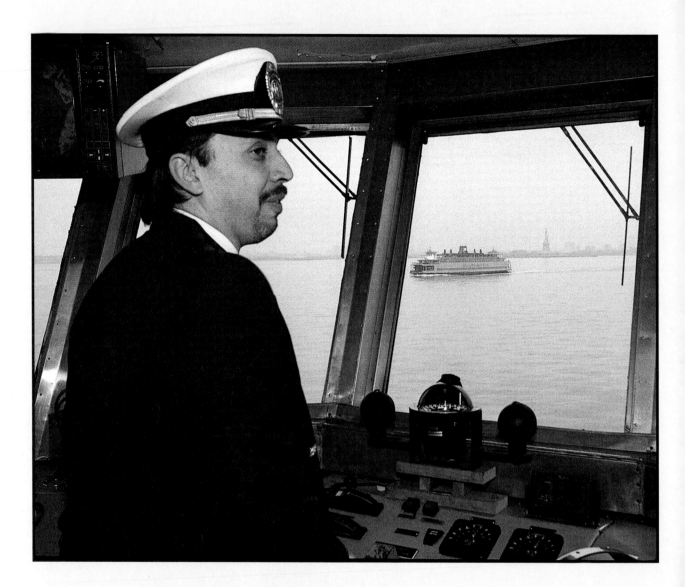

Captain Cruz watches these things each day on his way to and from the city.

23

Feel the ferry stop?
We have crossed the bay.

After every trip, and at the end of each day, Captain Cruz writes in the captain's log.
He records what happened along the way.

The captain does his job well.

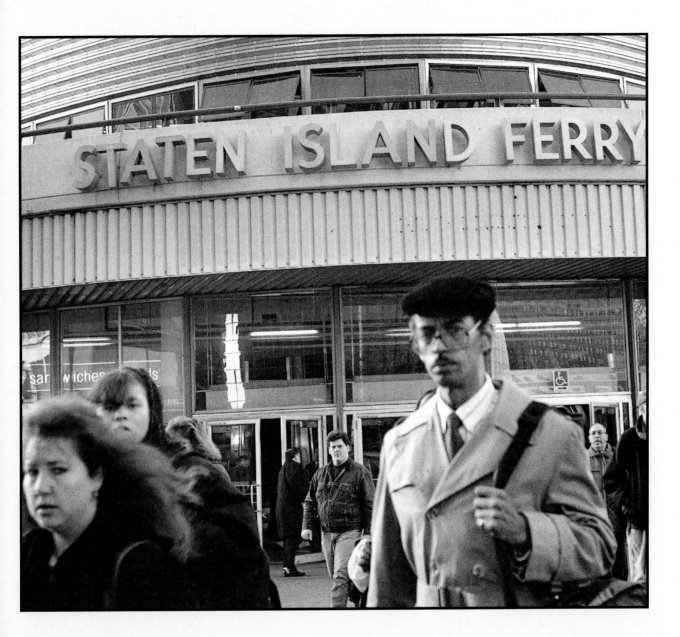

He helps people get to work
safely and on time.

Captain Cruz is careful
and responsible.

With hard work, he has made
his dream of being a ferryboat
captain come true!

Meet the Author
and the Photographer

Alice Flanagan and Christine Osinski are sisters. They grew up together telling stories and drawing pictures in a brown brick bungalow in a southwest-side neighborhood of Chicago, Illinois. Today they write stories and take photographs professionally.

Ms. Flanagan resides in Chicago with her husband and works as a freelance writer. Ms. Osinski is a photographer and teaches at The Cooper Union for the Advancement of Science and Art in New York City. She lives with her husband and two sons on Staten Island.

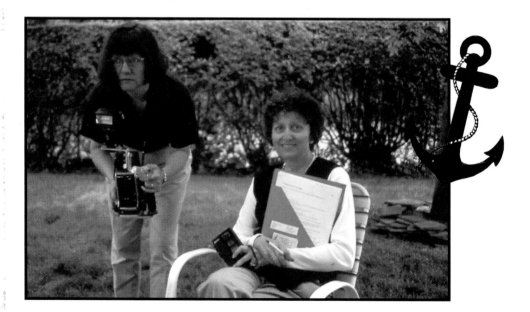